Yardbirds® make
going GREEN and making friends
the ultimate adventure!

Jenny Makes a Junkyard Friend

Written by Rich Kolb and Allison Aboud Holzer
Illustrated by Allison Aboud Holzer, M.A.T & M.F.A.

Jenny

from Venus?

nut

Jenny Makes a Junkyard Friend © 2008 The Bandana Co., Inc. Yardbirds®, the Yardbirds logo, and Junkyard® are registered trademarks of The Bandana Co., Inc. All rights reserved.

ISBN: 978-0-615-24574-4

BE CAREFUL. WARNING. Yardbirds® and Junkyard® sculptures are for decorative use only; they are not toys. They are made of metal. Some are quite heavy. Some are pointy. Do not touch without adult supervision. Thank you.

nut

D E D I C A T I O N

*To my beloved husband Paul for
making me laugh each day. Also, in memory
of my Ginni, my inspiration, who brightened
the spirits of everyone around her.*
—Allison

*For my loving mother – words can not express
my love and gratitude. You are my hero.*
—Rich

Jenny the puppy lived in a house that sat inside seven green rolling hills. Jenny loved using her imagination in new ways every day.

She dreamed of traveling with friends on an adventure, to help make the world a better place. But she had two big problems: first, she didn't have any friends and second, she didn't know how she could help make a difference.

One afternoon, Jenny spotted some giant flying balloons in the distance. She had never seen balloons like these before, and she thought maybe these balloons could take her around the world. So, she chased after them with an adventurous spirit, taking her much farther from home than she had ever been.

Jenny bounded across the blossoming hills until she suddenly ran into a big metal fence.

"Now I'll never catch those balloons!"
Jenny said, disappointed. Then she
noticed a hole in the fence. Peering
through a hole, she saw piles of junk.

"What is this place? I've never seen such
a mess." Her curiosity took over…

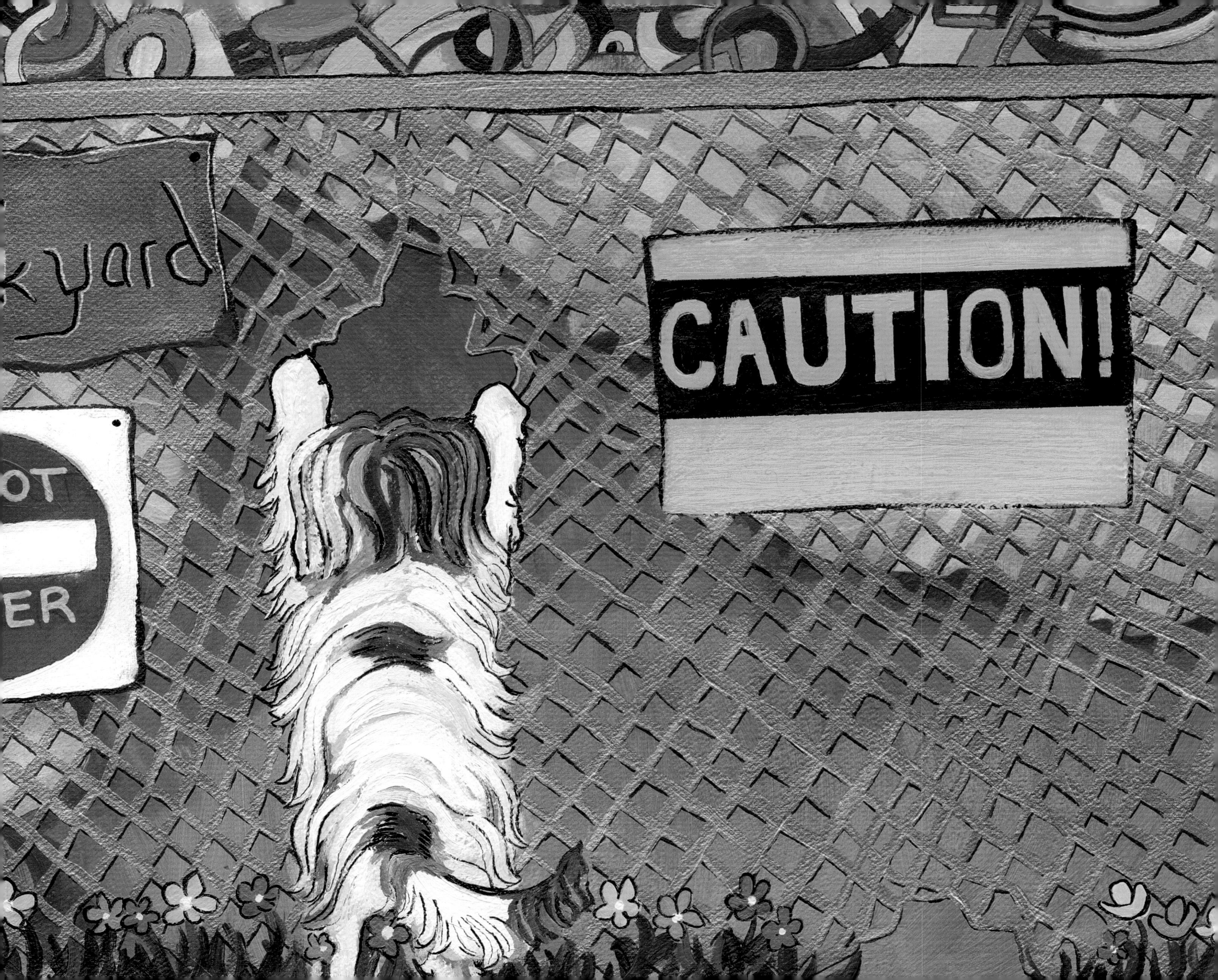
kyard
OT
ER
CAUTION!

wrench

...she wriggled herself through one of the holes to the other side of the fence.

Jenny had wandered into a giant junkyard maze. She began to make her way through twists and turns of tall metal piles. She marvelled at the shapes and colors in this junkyard world of thrown away things.

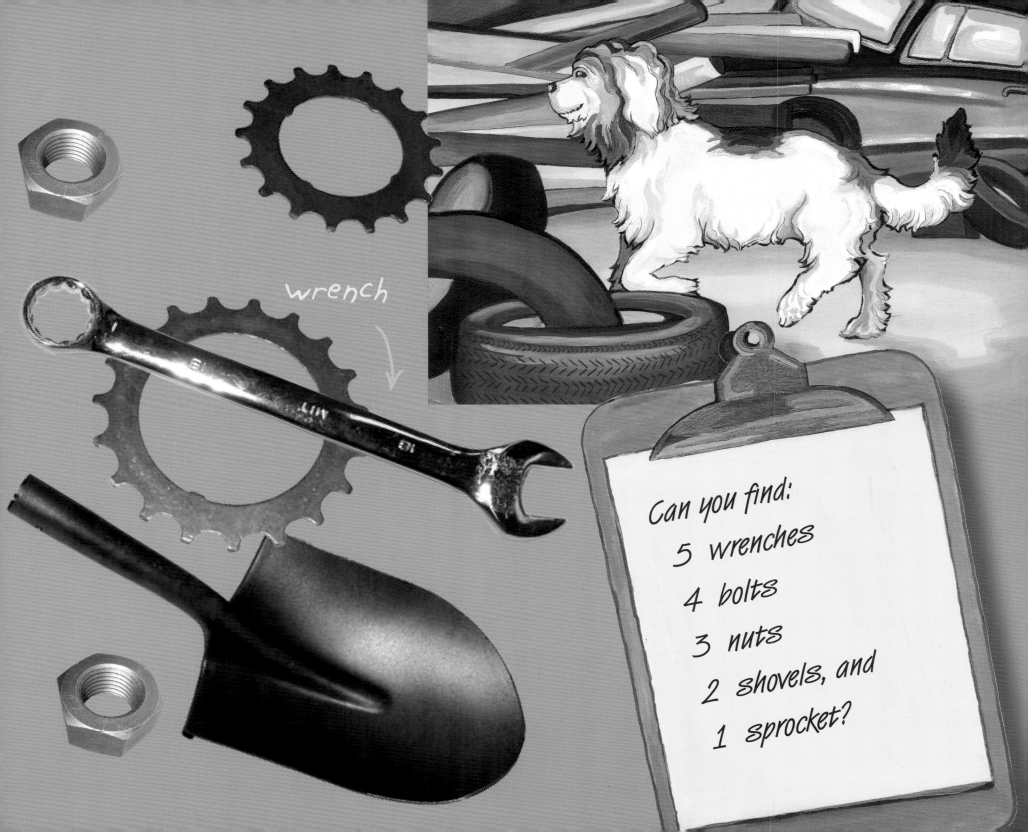

wrench

Can you find:
5 wrenches
4 bolts
3 nuts
2 shovels, and
1 sprocket?

"These huge piles of junk were once valuable things!" Jenny said, feeling sad. "I hope I never become useless and unwanted!"

Jenny's heart felt heavy as she thought of all this waste. Then, suddenly her imagination sparked! She pulled out junk pieces one-by-one – like bolts and shovels and wrenches and springs!

Can you find more parts?

On these pages?

Throughout the book?

"I've got it!!" Jenny shouted and started creating something with fast and furious focus.

She playfully matched different parts and pieces together. She tried many combinations.

Some worked and some didn't. She used her inventive spirit to keep going and her persistence paid off.

"I think I've got it!!" Jenny exclaimed. "All I need to do is tighten these bolts here…and attach a few more sprockets there…and…"

"Welcome
to the world,
my MOST wanted
Happy Puppy!"

Then, something
happened – Happy
Puppy wagged his
metal tail and said,
"Wow! The world sure
looks better from here."

"Thanks for helping
put my parts together
out of that jumbled
junkyard mess!"

Startled, Jenny bounced back: "Wh- wh-what did you SAY?"

"Well, I used to be parts from a car and a shovel. Now I'm a Happy Puppy thanks to you and your imagination!"

"Well, Happy Puppy, you're not junk parts anymore. You are a MOST wanted puppy and now my friend!"

Jenny was so grateful to have made a REAL Junkyard friend. And the two new friends jolly-romped and danced with joy!

But the puppy celebration quickly ended when Hank, the Crane Operator, walked up yelling, "Hey, you dogs - it's scat or get smashed! I'm about to compact all this junk!"

Jenny and Happy Puppy knew they had to run, but quickly they realized they were lost in the junkyard maze!

"Yikes!" said Jenny,
"We're lost!"

"Well, Jenny," said Happy Puppy,
"you made me from this junk,
right? Let's make another friend
who is wise and can fly up high to
find the fastest way out!"

So Happy Puppy and Jenny
made another useful
Junkyard friend.

"Welcome, Wise Old
Owl! Can you help
us? We need you
to fly up high over
the junkyard and find
the fastest way out before
the crane operator makes junk
patties out of us!"

Faster than a swinging crane, Wise
Old Owl zoomed up high to see.

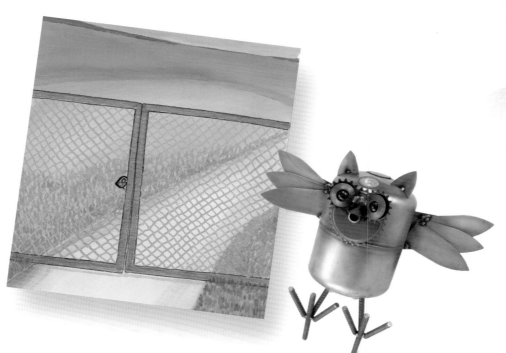

"Hi wily Monkey Wrench!
We need your help!

Following Wise Old Owl, can you
quickly swing through the junk,
climb the fence and open
the latch for us?"

"I see a locked gate nearby.
But we'll need wily fingers
to open it up! Wings or paws just
won't do! What do you think?"
Wise Old Owl said.

"Let's make a friend who can climb
quickly, who is agile and clever to
help us open that fence!"
Jenny exclaimed.

And so they began wrenching
some bolts and cans and rods
together.

Monkey said, "Oooh-oooh-oooh-Sure! Where?"

After Monkey wrenched open the fence, Owl thought a very wise thought: "I can fly and monkey can climb and swing with ease, but you puppies have to run all the way out through the long and twisting maze! Let's make a machine that will help carry you out of here with the greatest of speed!"

And so they started working with bicycle frames and wheels and garage door springs. They heard the crane engine starting just as they finished adding the last piece of their newest Junkyard creation…

Happy Puppy and Monkey Wrench hopped on their rockin' motorcycle ride, ready for a fast getaway!

Following Wise Old Owl, they sped through the maze, out past the fence, down the road and into the valley where more adventure awaited.

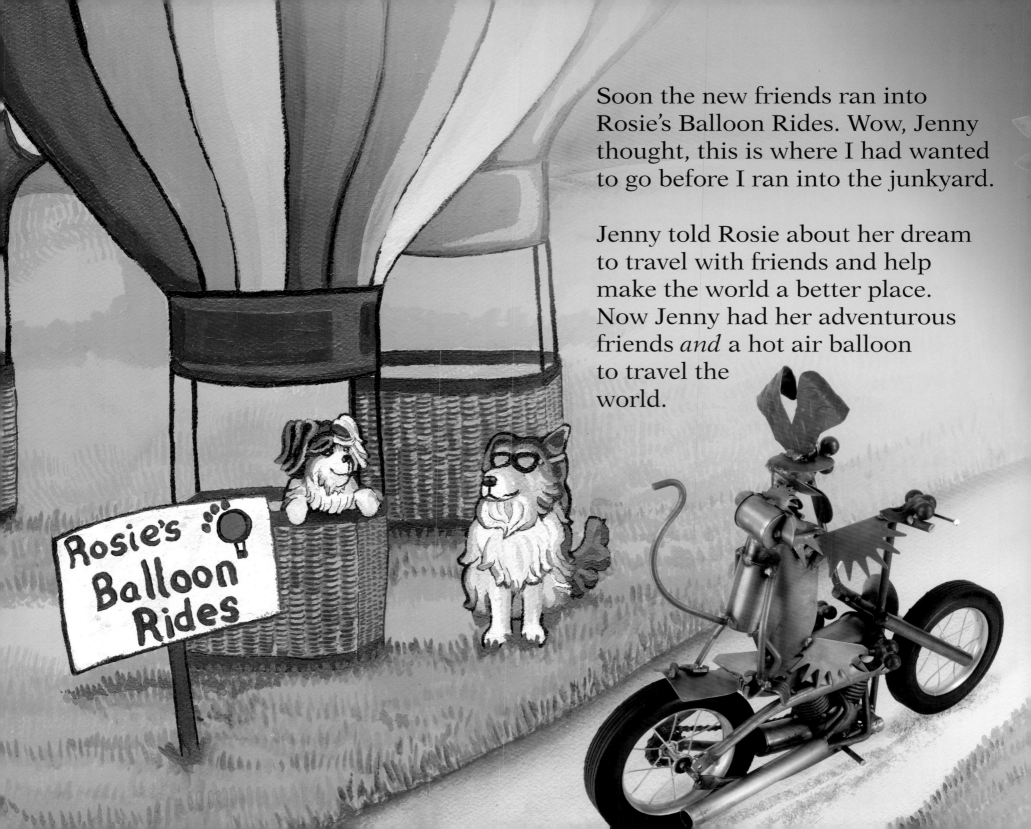

Soon the new friends ran into Rosie's Balloon Rides. Wow, Jenny thought, this is where I had wanted to go before I ran into the junkyard.

Jenny told Rosie about her dream to travel with friends and help make the world a better place. Now Jenny had her adventurous friends *and* a hot air balloon to travel the world.

Rosie's Balloon Rides

She had also
discovered a way
to help make the
world a better place
by recycling junk into useful
new things and fun new friends!

She wanted to share her new
discovery with the world!
Rosie smiled and said,
"I'm happy to help you,
as long as I can be
your puppy pilot!"

"Hop in, friends,
and hold on!" Rosie
shouted. "Heeerreee...
Weeeee... gooooo!!!!"

They soared up high over the junkyard.

They saw piles of junk down below in twisting, turning mazes of metal.

"Before I met all of you today, I knew I wanted to travel the world and make a difference, but I wasn't sure how! And now when I look down there, I don't see piles of useless things anymore. I see junkyards replaced with fields of flowers and fun new friends!" Jenny gratefully said.

"I see more rockin' motorcycles!" gggrrrruffed Happy Puppy.

"I see more acrobatic animals," said Monkey Wrench with a big, cheerful grin.

I see more acrobatic animals.

"And I see more balloon rides and friends of all kinds!" said Rosie.

"And I see a lot fewer junkyards filled with unwanted things," Jenny said.

And so Jenny and her friends embarked on a hot air balloon ride adventure to travel the world and to teach children how to recycle unwanted junk into wanted Junkyard® friends!

Join in the fun…
What would
you make?

THE
END
(for now!!)

Some more questions for you.

1. Can you find the Fried Chicken?

2. Which 2 critters are made from recycled bicycle chains?

3. Can you find the "Scaredy Cat"?

4. What did the Squirrel find?

5. Can you find the Poodle?

frying
pan

spring